Farmer Dale's Red Pickup Truck

WRITTEN BY
Lisa Wheeler

ILLUSTRATED BY
Ivan Bates

Harcourt, Inc.

Orlando   Austin   New York   San Diego   Toronto   London

www.HarcourtBooks.com

Library of Congress Cataloging-in-Publication Data
Wheeler, Lisa, 1963–
Farmer Dale's red pickup truck/Lisa Wheeler; illustrated by Ivan Bates.
p. cm.
Summary: One by one, Farmer Dale picks up animals who want a ride to
town in his rickety old pickup truck.
[1. Domestic animals—Fiction. 2. Pickup trucks—Fiction. 3. Trucks—
Fiction. 4. Stories in rhyme.] I. Bates, Ivan, ill. II. Title.
PZ8.3.W5668Far 2004
[E]—dc21   2003004987
ISBN 0-15-202319-4

First edition
A C E G H F D B

Manufactured in China

The illustrations in this book were done in
wax pencil crayons and watercolor on Fabriano paper.
The display type was hand lettered by Judythe Sieck.
The text type was set in Clearface.
Color separations by Bright Arts Ltd., Hong Kong
Manufactured by South China Printing Company, Ltd., China
This book was printed on totally chlorine-free Stora Enso Matte paper.
Production supervision by Sandra Grebenar and Pascha Gerlinger
Designed by Ivan Holmes

In memory of my mother, Barbara Budai Haroulakis,
who always made room, in her heart and her home, for more
—L. W.

For Jonah, Lorna, and Martin
—I. B.

Farmer Dale's red pickup truck
hauled a load of hay.
A bossy cow, with eyes of brown,
was standing in the way.

"How 'bout a ride?" asked Bossy Cow.

"Hop in," said Farmer Dale.

"Mooove over!" ordered Bossy Cow.

"There's no room for my tail."

The truck bounced up. The truck bounced down.
It spit and sputtered toward the town.

Farmer Dale's red pickup truck
was chugging right along.
A woolly sheep came strolling by,
bleating out a song.

"Room for more?" sang Woolly Sheep.
"Fit me in somehow?"
"No problem," answered Farmer Dale.
"Mooove over!" uttered Cow.

The truck bounced up and shimmied.
It coughed and wheezed back down.

The pickup spit a cloud of smoke
and sputtered toward the town.

Farmer Dale's red pickup truck
hit a rocky bump.
It swerved beside a roly pig,
skating past the dump.

"Oh, my stars!" squealed Roly Pig.
"You folks just knocked me down."
"So sorry," Dale apologized.
"Need a ride to town?"
"I do indeed," said Roly Pig.
"My skates are broken now."
"Climb aboard," sang Woolly Sheep.
"Mooove over!" ordered Cow.

The truck bounced up and groaned back down.
It hiccuped twice and chugged toward town.

Farmer Dale's red pickup truck
slowly rattled on.
A goat with an accordion
stood grazing on the lawn.
"Can I squeeze in?" asked Nanny Goat.
"My pleasure," Farmer said.

"Ba-a-a-d idea," sang Woolly Sheep.

"The engine's almost dead."

"No room!" lamented Roly Pig.

"We're overcrowded now!"

"We'll make some room," said Farmer Dale.

"Mooove over!" bossed the cow.

The truck bounced up. The springs all popped.
The bumper bumped. The pickup stopped.

Farmer Dale's red pickup truck
stood stranded in the road.
"It seems you have a problem,"
a cocky rooster crowed.

"We do," admitted Farmer Dale.
"The problem is we're stuck.
The weight of all these animals
is too much for my truck."
Rooster eyed the animals.
"You're such a cozy group.
I hate to cluck like Mother Hen,
but who will fly the coop?"

"I just squeezed in," said Nanny Goat.

"I'm faint," squealed Roly Pig.

"I won't mooove," said Bossy Cow.

"I'm boss of this red rig."

"Too ba-a-a-d for you," sang Woolly Sheep.

"The biggest has to go."

"Settle down," said Farmer Dale.

"Let's think now—nice and slow."

"I'll get out," the farmer said,
"and push us from the rear."
"Good idea," said Nanny Goat.
 Cow replied, "I'll steer."
 Farmer Dale's red pickup truck
 didn't budge at all.
 Dale pushed until his face was red,
 and then he heard a call.

"Can I butt in?" asked Nanny Goat.
"I'd like to lend a hoof."
Rooster squawked, "I'll point the way,"
then roosted on the roof.

"I'll pitch in," sang Woolly Sheep.
"I'll ra-a-a-m it with my head."
"Don't hog the fun," said Roly Pig.
"Let's all help out, instead."

The pickup rocked and rumbled.
It rolled an inch or so.
"It's moooving!" shouted Bossy Cow.
The rooster crowed, "Too slow!"
"Turn the key," said Farmer Dale.
"I can't!" the cow replied.
"She's got no ha-a-a-nds,"
 explained the sheep.
 Farmer Dale just sighed.

"You should steer," said Bossy Cow.
"We'll mooove this heap along."
The beasts all pushed together
and sang a working song.

The pickup bounced and shimmied.
It groaned and squeaked and wheezed.
It spit a thankful cloud of smoke
and started with a sneeze.

Farmer Dale's red pickup truck
rumbled into town,
hauling Goat and Pig and Sheep,
and Cow with eyes of brown.
Rooster roosting on the hood
cried, "Cock-a-doodle-cluck!"

'Hip-hooray for Farmer Dale
and his red pickup truck!'